SCIENCE FAIR!

by Ellen Garin illustrated by Molly Delaney

Harcourt

Orlando   Boston   Dallas   Chicago   San Diego

Visit *The Learning Site!*

www.harcourtschool.com

It was Monday morning at Carver Elementary School. There was a buzz of excitement outside Ms. Bale's classroom. All the kids were looking at something on the door. "What could it be?" Colin wondered. He tried to see over everyone's head.

It was no use. Colin was the shortest kid in the class. The bell rang. Everyone went into the classroom. Colin read the poster on the classroom door.

"Class Science Fair Next Week! Fun Projects! Think Like A Scientist! All Welcome!"

"A science fair," Colin thought. "That sounds exciting!" He walked into the classroom and sat down.

"Good morning, class," said Ms. Bale. "We are going to try something new. We will try thinking like scientists."

Ms. Bale wrote these words on the board: *Problem, Idea, Solution.*

"A scientist is a problem solver," Ms. Bale said. "The scientist sees a problem. The scientist looks for an idea. The idea is a way to solve the problem. An idea that works is called a solution."

Colin listened carefully to Ms. Bale.

"Each of you will do a project," Ms. Bale said. "First, you will tell about a problem. Next, you will look for ideas. Then, you will tell about the solution."

Henson raised his hand. "What about the science fair?"

Ms. Bale smiled. "You will show your projects at the fair. You will have until Friday to do your projects."

"Good!" Colin thought. "I have plenty of time to think of an idea!"

"Now, please hand in your homework," Ms. Bale said.

Colin looked in his backpack. "Oh no!" he thought. "I hope I didn't forget my homework!" Colin looked again, but his homework was not in his backpack.

"Colin, where is your homework?" Ms. Bale asked.

"I left it at home, Ms. Bale," said Colin.

"Well, please bring it in tomorrow," said Ms. Bale.

"Yes, Ms. Bale," said Colin.

Colin sighed. He hoped his day would get better.

At lunch, everyone talked about the science fair. Adria and Hannah would work together. Matt and Henson were going to work with Miko. Kris and Ruth were also a team. A few people would work alone. Colin did not want to work alone. He wanted to work with someone, too.

Colin thought and thought. Who could he work with?

Then Colin noticed that he had accidentally knocked over his juice. His sandwich was soaked! Colin put the sandwich back in the plastic bag. He stuffed the bag into his backpack.

"Colin, do you want some of my sandwich?" Alex asked.

"No, but thank you for asking," Colin said. Then Colin had a great idea.

"Alex, will you work with me on a project for the science fair?" asked Colin.

"Okay," said Alex.

"We'll be a great team!" Colin said.

After school, Alex and Colin walked home together. They talked about the science fair.

"Let's think of ideas for our project," Colin said. We have to think of something that will solve a problem."

"How about a robot?" Alex asked.

"That's been done," Colin said. "What are some problems that need solutions?"

The boys walked on. They couldn't come up with an idea.

"I guess we will think of something," Colin said. Alex nodded.

"See you tomorrow," Alex said and waved goodbye.

Colin was worried that they couldn't think of a problem. Maybe the science fair wouldn't be fun after all!

When Colin got home, his mom was in the kitchen. She was sitting at the kitchen table reading.

"What's wrong, Colin?" she asked.

"I have had the worst day!" Colin said. "I forgot my homework. I spilled juice on my sandwich. Worst of all, Alex and I can't think of an idea for our science project." Colin frowned and sat down next to his mom.

Colin's mom smiled and reached over to give him a hug. "Don't worry," she said. "I'm sure you will think of something."

"I hope so," Colin said and hugged his mom again.

Colin took his backpack up to his room and sat at his desk. He liked to sit in this spot and look out the window whenever he had a bad day. He could see the birds in the trees. Cars passed by on the street below. The neighbor's dog tossed a ball into the air and caught it. "The science fair is on Friday," Colin thought. "Maybe I'll have an idea tomorrow."

The next day, Ms. Bale brought many things to class.

On a table were empty soda bottles and paper plates. There were sheets of newspaper. There were cups. There was a small box of paper clips. There were drinking straws and string. There were wire coat hangers. There was a box of rubber bands.

"You will learn some new things today," said Ms. Bale.

The class put paper cups to their ears. The cups made sounds louder. They used a magnifying glass. It made things look bigger. Ms. Bale put out some science books. The books showed simple projects.

"You can choose one of these projects," said Ms. Bale, "or come up with an idea of your own. Write your name on this paper," she said. "Write the name of your project, too."

Ms. Bale posted the list on the wall. Everyone wanted to be the first to sign up.

"We're making the telephone!"

"We're making the book band!"

"We're making the whirlybird airplane!"

Once again, Colin was at the end of the line. And once again, he struggled to see the list. Soon everyone had a project except Colin and Alex.

"What should we do?" Alex asked.

Colin thought for a minute. He remembered the bad day he had the day before. He remembered not being able to see the list. Then he had an idea.

"I've got it!" Colin said. He whispered his idea to Alex. Alex's face brightened.

"Now that's a problem that needs to be solved!" Alex said.

The rest of the week, Alex and Colin worked on their project at Colin's house.

They finished the project Thursday night. "I thought we would never finish," Alex said.

"I can't wait to show it at the science fair tomorrow!" said Colin.

Colin and Alex knew that their project would be different from the other projects.

On Friday, the teams brought their projects to the science fair.

Matt, Henson, and Miko showed their paper cup scales. They filled the cups with pennies to balance them on a hanger.

Kris and Ruth's paper clip airplane was very popular. It went around and around. Everyone wanted to try the paper clip airplane.

Adria and Hannah set up their water magnifying glass. The girls explained how the drop of water magnified small things.

Then it was Colin and Alex's turn.

"Our problem was how to make a bad day better," Colin said. "On Monday I had a bad day. It all started because I was too short to see the science fair poster. I forgot my homework. I spilled juice on my sandwich. But this box solves all of those problems," Colin said.

The boys pulled out their science project—a long narrow box. It looked like several juice cartons taped together.

Colin stood on the box to make himself taller. "Now I can see a sign on the door." Colin opened the box and pulled out his homework. "I can keep my homework in here so I don't forget it." Colin put the box on the table and put a bottle of juice against it. "And this box will keep my juice from spilling."

Alex and Colin smiled at each other. Their one idea solved three problems!